ALSO AVAILABLE IN THIS SERIES

Anne Arrives

Anne's Kindred Spirits

Anne's School Days

Anne's
TRAGICAL TEA PARTY

To my favorite tea-drinking kindred spirit, Tiffany —K.G.

For Madeleine Jean —A.H.

With undying gratitude to L.M. Montgomery for creating the classic story on which this book is based.

Text copyright © 2022 by Kallie George
Illustrations copyright © 2022 by Abigail Halpin

Tundra Books, an imprint of Penguin Random House Canada Young Readers,
a division of Penguin Random House of Canada Limited

Library and Archives Canada Cataloguing in Publication

Title: Anne's tragical tea party / adapted by Kallie George ; pictures by Abigail Halpin.
Names: George, K. (Kallie), 1983- author. | Halpin, Abigail, illustrator. | Adaptation of (work):
   Montgomery, L. M. (Lucy Maud), 1874-1942. Anne of Green Gables.
Series: George, K. (Kallie), 1983- Anne chapter book ; 3.
Description: Series statement: An Anne chapter book ; 3
Identifiers: Canadiana (print) 20200383485 | Canadiana (ebook) 20200383523 |
   ISBN 9780735267220 (hardcover) | ISBN 9780735267237 (EPUB)
Subjects: LCGFT: Fiction.
Classification: LCC PS8563.E6257 A85 2022 | DDC jC813/.6—dc23

Published simultaneously in the United States of America by Tundra Books of Northern New York,
an imprint of Penguin Random House Canada Young Readers, a division of Penguin Random House of Canada Limited

Library of Congress Control Number: 2020949586

Acquired by Tara Walker
Edited by Peter Phillips
Designed by Kate Sinclair
The artwork in this book was rendered in graphite, watercolor and colored pencil, and completed digitally.
The text was set in Fournier.

Printed in China

www.penguinrandomhouse.ca

1   2   3   4   5   26   25   24   23   22

Penguin
Random House
TUNDRA BOOKS

INSPIRED BY ANNE OF GREEN GABLES

Anne's
TRAGICAL TEA PARTY

ADAPTED BY
KALLIE GEORGE

PICTURES BY
ABIGAIL HALPIN

tundra

CHAPTER 1

Anne Shirley danced through the door of Green Gables. Her arms were full of branches covered in colorful leaves.

"I found these in the woods where Diana and I have pretend tea parties," said Anne. "I am going to decorate my room with them. Don't they look beautiful?"

Marilla frowned. "They look messy. Mind you don't drop leaves everywhere."

Marilla and Matthew Cuthbert had adopted Anne in the last year, but already Anne had caused *years'* worth of trouble.

"If only Anne would act a little more sensibly," thought Marilla.

That gave her an idea.

"Now listen, Anne," said Marilla. "I'll be away at a meeting at the Aid Society today. So . . . I've decided you can ask Diana over for tea, to keep you company and out of mischief."

"Oh, Marilla!" Anne clasped her hands. "How perfectly lovely and grown-uppish!"

"Yes, exactly," said Marilla. "It is a good chance for you to practice your manners."

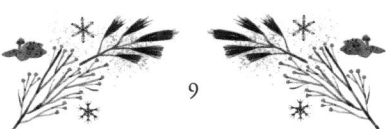

Anne had spent a lot of time looking after
other children when she was an orphan.
She had never had a real tea party before.
Or a real best friend.

Now she couldn't imagine life without Diana.
And she couldn't believe her luck. Marilla was
letting her have a *real* tea party! Anne felt bad
that she was always getting into trouble.
This was the perfect chance to show Marilla
that she really could be grown-up!

"May I use the rosebud tea set?" Anne asked.

"Most certainly not," said Marilla. "The plain one will do. But there is a half-bottle of raspberry cordial in the pantry you may have as a treat."

Anne was thrilled.

Raspberry cordial! The sweet red juice looked so beautiful. And it tasted divine.

She couldn't wait!

CHAPTER 2

Anne ran to tell Diana, who lived nearby at Orchard Slope.

Diana was just as thrilled. But her mother, Mrs. Barry, was not. Mrs. Barry was even stricter than Marilla. She was not sure that Anne was a suitable friend for her daughter.

Still, Anne and Diana couldn't get into trouble at a tea party . . . could they?

In the early afternoon, as soon as Marilla left, Diana came over to Green Gables, all dressed up. Anne answered the door, all dressed up too.

She shook hands with Diana, just like a grown-up would.

"How is your mother?" Anne asked, even though she had seen Mrs. Barry that morning.

"She is very well, thank you," replied Diana.

Anne and Diana giggled.

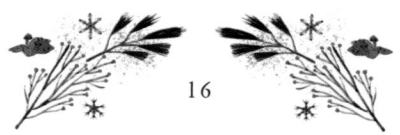

"Let's start with some raspberry cordial," said Anne. "Then we can have some tea."

She went to the pantry but couldn't see the bottle at first. Eventually, she found it on the top shelf. She hurried back and poured Diana a glass.

It was so fun to pretend to be a grown-up.

Diana sipped daintily. "Oh, it's awfully nice," she said, and she finished her cup. "It's the nicest raspberry cordial I've ever had!"

"Here, have another," said Anne.

Anne poured Diana a second glass, and Diana drank that up as well. Anne was so busy talking, she didn't drink any herself.

Anne poured Diana some more, then went to set out the cookies and make the tea. "There are *so* many responsibilities when you are a grown-up," she said to herself.

When Anne got back, Diana was frowning.

"What's the matter?" asked Anne worriedly.

"I don't feel well. I — I'm awfully sick,"
said Diana.

"But we haven't had our tea yet,"
said Anne.

"I — I need to go home," said Diana.

She stood up. Right away, Anne could see that Diana was dizzy.

Anne quickly fetched Diana's hat and then helped her back to Orchard Slope.

Poor Diana! Anne hoped she would feel better soon.

So much for having fun. The tea party had gone tragically!

CHAPTER 3

Anne didn't know just *how* tragically the tea
party had gone until the next day.

When Marilla found out that Diana was sick,
she marched to the pantry and came back
with some answers.

"You gave Diana currant wine instead of
cordial!" said Marilla.

Currant wine? That was meant only for
grown-ups. No wonder Diana was sick!

Anne burst into tears.

"Oh, Anne," said Marilla. "You certainly have a genius for getting into trouble. Couldn't you tell that it wasn't cordial?"

"I didn't drink any," cried Anne. "I was too busy talking."

Marilla sighed. Her plan to help Anne be sensible had gone wrong. But now that Marilla thought on it, the mix-up wasn't all Anne's fault.

"I told you that the cordial was in the pantry, but it was actually in the cellar. There, there." Marilla patted Anne's shoulder. "I will go over and explain to Mrs. Barry that it was all a mistake."

And that's just what Marilla did.

But Mrs. Barry didn't believe Marilla.
She thought Anne had gotten Diana sick on
purpose. She also thought Marilla was being
too soft on Anne.

Marilla came home, snappish and scowling.

So Anne went to see Mrs. Barry herself.

Mrs. Barry answered the door stiffly.

Anne clasped her hands as hard as she could. "Please, *please* forgive me," she said. "Diana is my bosom friend."

"No," said Mrs. Barry. "You cannot play with Diana anymore. Now go home and behave yourself."

That night, Anne cried herself to sleep. She was in the depths of despair.

What was life without a bosom friend?

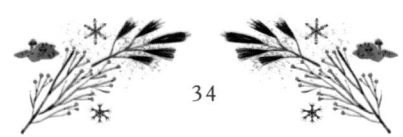

CHAPTER 4

At school the next day, Diana slipped Anne
a letter.

Dear Anne,

Mother says I'm not to play with you.
Please don't be mad at me. I love you as
much as ever!

I made you a new bookmark out of red tissue
paper. When you look at it, remember your
true friend.

Diana Barry

Anne wrote back:

Darling Diana,

I am not cross at you. I shall keep your lovely present forever. You are my busum friend. Please excuse mistakes because my spelling isn't very good yet, although much improoved.

Yours until death us do part,

Anne Shirley

Their letters made Anne feel a bit better. But it still felt like her life was covered in a dark cloud of woe.

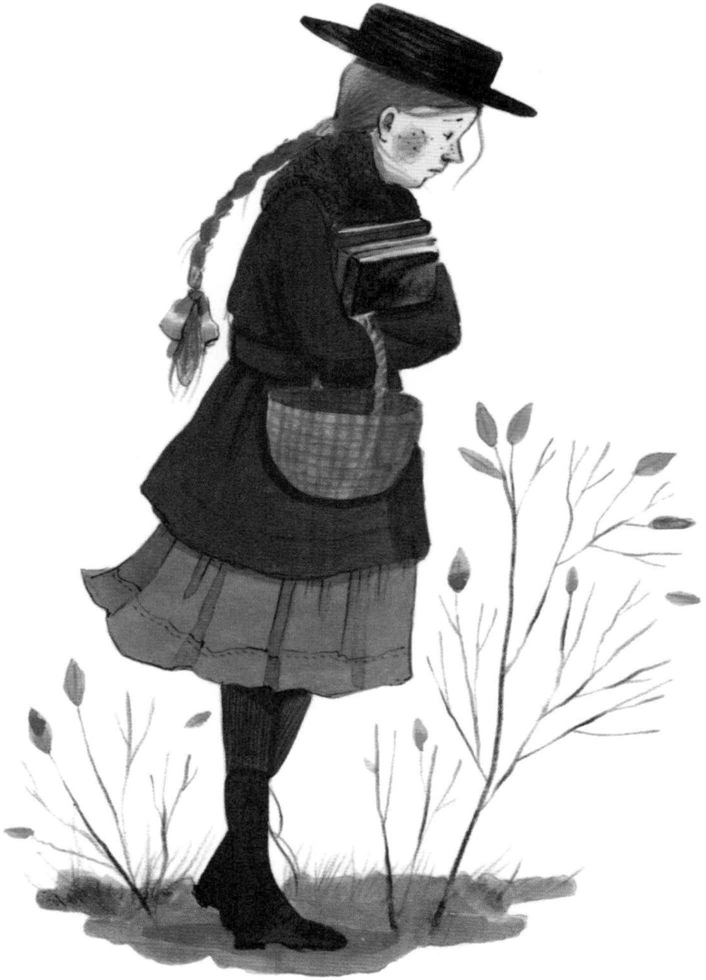

"Please bury me with this bookmark," Anne told Marilla that night. "I don't believe I'll live very long. Perhaps when Mrs. Barry sees me at my funeral, she might forgive me then."

"I don't think you will die of grief as long as you can talk," said Marilla.

Secretly though, Marilla wished Mrs. Barry would see the truth. Anne might cause mischief, but she never meant wrong.

CHAPTER 5

Marilla was right. Anne couldn't stay completely sad in such an interesting world. Still, Anne missed Diana very much.

She slept with Diana's letter under her pillow.

Then, one snowy night in January, Anne didn't sleep at all . . .

Marilla was away again at another meeting. Anne and Matthew were enjoying a cozy fire when the kitchen door was flung open.

Diana stood there, breathless.

"My little sister, Minnie May, is awfully sick. Mother and Father are away in town. Oh, Anne! I don't know what to do," cried Diana.

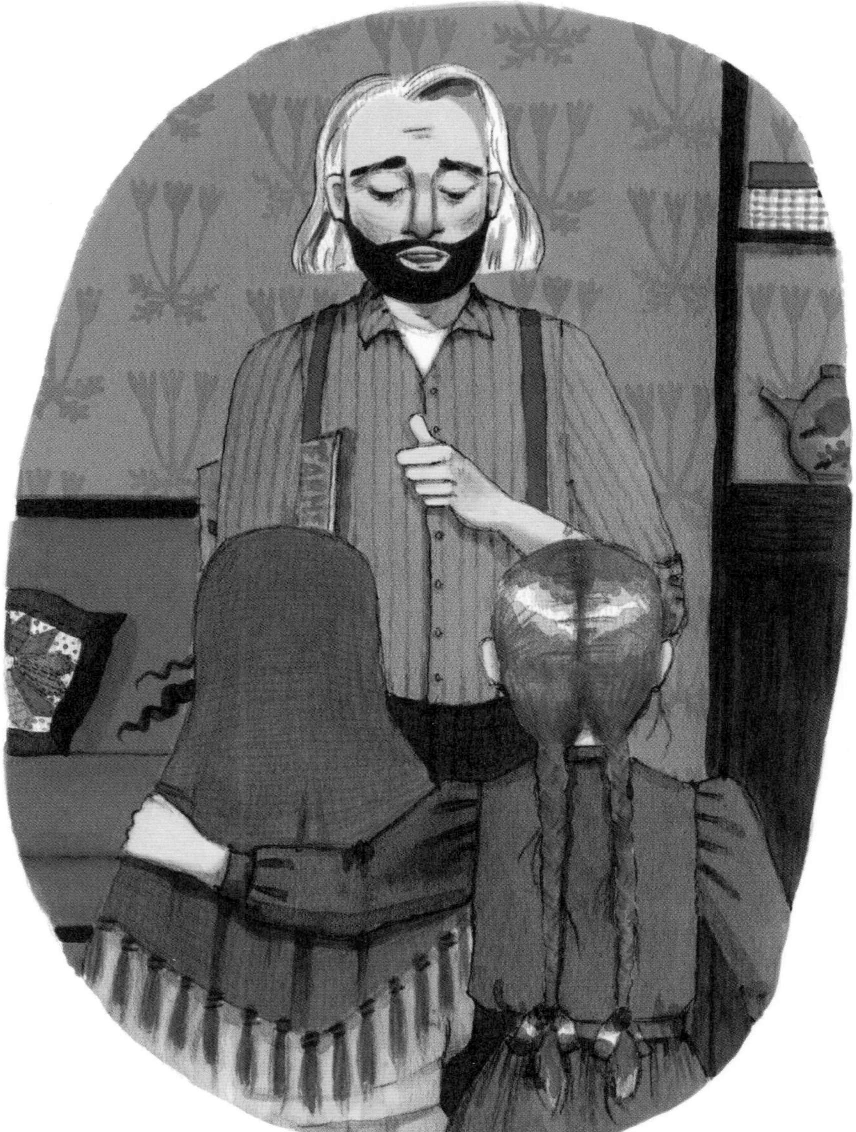

For once, Anne didn't speak.

Quiet Matthew spoke first. "I will go for the doctor."

"But the doctor is so far away," said Diana. "What will we do until then?"

Anne leapt into action. She had looked after many sick children before being adopted by Marilla and Matthew.

"Matthew will be as quick as he can. Meanwhile, I can help. Take me to Minnie May," said Anne.

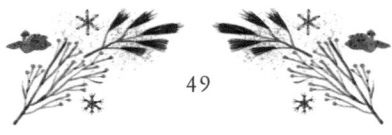

Together they hurried back to
Orchard Slope. It was very beautiful
out, but Anne didn't notice the starry,
sparkly snow. She was thinking only
of Minnie May.

CHAPTER 6

Minnie May was tossing and turning with fever.

"Oh, Anne. It's really bad, isn't it?" stammered Diana.

"Yes," said Anne. "But I have seen worse." That wasn't true. But Anne didn't want to worry Diana even more.

Anne went right to work. She gave
Minnie May some water and broth.
She put damp towels on Minnie May's
forehead. Diana helped too. But Anne
was the one in charge.

Anne worked all night long.

When Matthew and the doctor got there,
the worst was over.

Anne was too exhausted for words. So was
Diana. But they hugged each other tightly.

Anne had saved Minnie May's life.

CHAPTER 7

Anne slept all the next day. When she finally woke up, it was the afternoon. Marilla had news.

"Mrs. Barry wants to see you, Anne," said Marilla.

Anne sprang to her feet. She ran all the way to Orchard Slope. Could it be what she had hoped for?

Yes!

Soon Anne came dancing back to
Green Gables.

"Oh, Marilla!" she exclaimed. "Mrs. Barry
cried and kissed me. I can see Diana whenever
I want! Mrs. Barry said she was sorry for not
believing me before. Then we had tea, with
their best tea set. Everything was *so* elegant.
It must be lovely to be a grown-up."

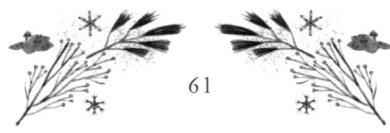

"Well, I don't know about that," said Marilla.

But Marilla did know one thing, which clearly Mrs. Barry now knew too.

Anne might be imaginative, and talkative, and even a bit of trouble, but when it mattered most, she was the most practical and sensible of all.

"I am so proud of you, Anne," Marilla added.

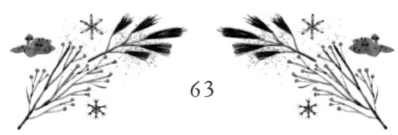

Matthew nodded.

Anne was proud as well. "You know, when I *am* a grown-up, I will never keep bosom friends apart. Or laugh at little girls who use big words. But . . ."

She stopped, thinking of the night before. "For now, I'd like to keep being a little girl." She looked at Marilla and Matthew. *"Your* little girl, here at Green Gables."

"We would like that too," said Marilla. "Very, *very* much."

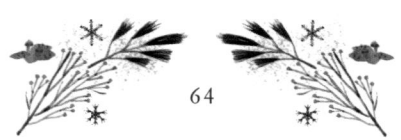